Claudine and the Bridge of Two Hearts

Claudine and the Bridge of Two Hearts

by Marian Grudko *and* T.A. Young

Claudine illustrations by Donal Partelow

Cover painting by Renée Gauvin

138 in Progress Publishing
New York

Claudine and the Bridge of Two Hearts

Copyright © 2024 Marian Grudko and T.A. Young

All rights reserved, including the right of reproduction in whole or in part in any form.

This is a work of fiction. Any references to historical events, real people or real places are used fictitiously. Other names, characters, places and events are products of the authors' imaginations and any resemblance to actual events or places or persons, living or dead, is entirely coincidental.

Published by 138 In Progress Publishing, Dover Plains, New York.
www.138inprogresspublishing.com
mariangrudko@138inprogresspublishing.com

Claudine Illustration © 2024 Donal Partelow
donalpartelow@gmail.com

First Edition: November 2024
Printed in the United States of America

Library of Congress Control Number: 2024914832
ISBN: 979-8-9911008-0-9

Cover painting by Renée Gauvin
@reneegauvinart

Book formatted by Elliot Toman

For Andria and Todd,
and for Arthur.

- M.G.

For Andria, Victoria, Taylor, Davy, and Julia.
You have made me the luckiest man on the planet.

- T.A.Y.

Nature never did betray the heart that loved her.
  - Wordsworth, "Tintern Abbey"

A Few Words Before We Begin

A moth, who spoke perfect Parisian French, told me that he knew Claudine. This was plausible; his clothes were pure chic.

"Yes," said Claudine, over the transatlantic phone, "he is telling the truth. We met in Paris... I was new to the city and lonely, and attracted to his style... Alas, after coffee and *croissants* I found him earnest, but not very bright. Too many street lamp concussions, I presumed. The relationship went nowhere."

The moth - his name is Henri - asked me how our ladybug was faring. He had read our first book, but was not clear about what happened before her film opened.

We were about to tell him the story when he begged us to wait, as it was close to his bed time, but could we perhaps record the events in a second book?

We did not have to be asked twice. Here is our tale, for all of you, who, despite - or because of - any headlong encounters with lampposts - are eager to read more about Claudine.

As our friend, Fabienne Ruiz, wrote:

"*Une coccinelle est toujours un morceau de bonheur...*"

"A ladybug is always a bit of happiness..."

One
CLAUDINE

Claudine sat at her dressing table, regarding herself in the mirror, adjusting her pearls. A ladybug, not so young as when she first made her way to Paris, but still ravishing.

The painting on the wall was of a distraught human woman, by the American artist, Stacie Flint. Ordinarily, Claudine was not interested in portraits unless they were of herself, but this one had disturbed her enough to buy it. She was perturbed by the title: "The Beauty Slave's Quest for Serenity". Surely Ms. Flint needed counsel? was Claudine's first thought. Then a doubt entered her mind: was she, herself, such a slave?

It was in Auvers-sur-Oise, a short train ride from Paris, that Claudine first lived and dreamed. To her, the gardens were bouquets thrown at her feet; the tall tree, *le Tour Eiffel*, from which all could see her; and her reflection in ponds lit by countless fireflies was surely herself on the silver screen. Ah, she needed to live in Paris, to experience that *beau monde*, as much as the city clearly needed her.

One day, Claudine begged to speak with her mother about a dream she had, the very one we have read.

Madame Pompea Coccinelle was seated at her writing desk. She set down her quill and turned to her child. "My daughter, you are a ladybug, but first, a lady. Transformation is in your blood and in your soul. The flame must never be extinguished: go where your heart and your wings take you. And if your wings aren't enough, a locomotive will serve. Most importantly, never forget your home, that it is both small as this fern, and as vast as this forest. And remember: *ma chère*, you shall always be Claudine."

Claudine went to Paris and took the city by storm. Model, fashion designer, actress - was there anything she could not do? She was assisted by Pierre, a sometime-rooster who lived mostly in human form and who had transformed her into what she thought she needed to be. But Claudine in human form had not been happy. Choosing to be herself, with her own six legs, she created new clothes, wore multiple pairs of Christian Louboutins, and was now starring in a motion picture which would hit the Parisian theaters in less than three weeks.

"I have arrived," said Claudine to her reflection in the mirror. It should have been a rapturous moment, to be shared with Pierre. Instead, she left her apartment and walked alone along the Seine.

Standing in the middle of a bridge, she contemplated the events of yesterday.

Two
Yesterday: The Luncheon

The taxi stopped at l'Hotel du Centre Paris. There she would meet a circle of new human friends – inexplicably acquired – who were laden with jewels and titles, and attired in material that was clearly allergic to imperfections of any kind.

Yet it was they who acted impressed; they practically showed movement when she stopped before their table. In this echelon, where the bend of a finger can be judged and sentenced to eternal banishment, movement is something measured with seismographs.

"Claudine! Such a pleasure!" said Baroness de Laurie. Before she could lower herself to her chair, waiters appeared from all directions to fill glasses, to open napkins, and to bow almost acrobatically.

After a splendid lunch, during which the ladies noticed Claudine's unusual diet of honey, raisins, and some sort of white caviar, Countess Mesantier sighed, "And now comes Spring."

"Why, Countess, would you regret Spring?" asked Claudine. "The flowers and leaves awaken! The ponds, so still all winter, are now...."

The Countess cut her off: "Yes, trees and birds. Our estate is positively brimming with them. Acres and acres of these things. But the pests! They come out from wherever it is they wintered. Vile creatures."

"Pests?"

"You know: those ubiquitous bugs, ants, spiders, flies, moths, mosquitoes, beetles...."

"But aren't they, aren't they...."

"They are, dear Claudine, pests. We have a team of exterminators who dig and spray for all manner of these insidious creatures so we may enjoy nature as it is meant to be: undisturbed, unblemished, cleansed. Nature is meant to be pure and perfect, not a game of swatting flies and pinching gnats."

Claudine thought of her friends, her list sounding remarkably like that of the Countess. Recalling them, she said half-aloud, "My friends."

Those at the table were touched by the intimate way she said the words. They felt welcomed by her. She had made her way into their circle. A fortuitous misunderstanding.

But the truth was so sad, she had to force herself to look up into the sedate smiling faces before her.

"Where," she asked herself, "Where am I? Where do I

Chapter II

belong? Am I one of those 'pests'? A beetle?"

Funny, how the ground can seem so unsteady, even when the legs of your chair are exactly the same length and the floor perfect. Claudine the Ladybug was awakened from a spell. She gently took a sip of water and fought her own retreat.

Three
THE BRIDGE

Claudine stood on the Bridge of Two Hearts, as indecisive as anyone who finds herself simultaneously so lost and so found. For the first time since she arrived in Paris, her inclination was toward her home in Auvers, her pastoral home. She was wounded by the luncheon, and wondered what it was about the human world that had captivated her for so long.

It was indeed a team of humans who were about to make her a movie star. And she could shrug off the luncheon, blaming the pitiable blindness of those particular ladies. She knew the real problem: Know Thyself. Claudine asked, "What am I to do? How do I know what to do if I don't know what matters? Why must I have every creature see me, admire me, like me?" She thought of that one pair of eyes that saw her and genuinely knew who she was: Pierre. What would he say? And what species would

Chapter III

he be speaking from? Or for?

She could do what most of the universe did: just let the motion, the wind and waves of destiny, take her where she was meant to be. But this was not Claudine.

Pierre approached her from 'the other' side of the bridge. She saw him, and glowed a brighter red, and vibrated with the smallest particle of trepidation. How can something so small, almost invisible, have so much presence?

Sometimes, the small-but-great can be interrupted by the great-but-small. This was Emilie's cue.

On that bridge, as Pierre and Claudine looked down at the noncommittal waters, Emilie found whom she had been seeking, one she knew back in the day of leaves and petals, her friend Claudine.

Emilie had not been a true friend to Claudine. She was one of the ladybugs who mocked Claudine's dreams of Paris, though Emilie had some terrific stories herself (the kind of stuff that gave Ovid his following). She landed on the stone wall.

Claudine was so shaken, she immediately lost some of her color. Pierre was not surprised. He knew the cause of her sudden change. He folded his hands together and leaned against the bridge with the patience typical of neither man nor rooster, but a creature who knew a great deal about the worlds of both.

After the embrace, Claudine saw that Emilie had only five legs.

"What happened?" she asked.

Emilie shrugged. "A close call with a beak." (Pierre took no offense.) She smiled and said, "But I hear you have been doing very well with just two. Makes me wonder why we were given six."

Pierre couldn't help but cut in: "Six allows for more close calls." The ladybugs nodded: a lot of wisdom in that.

There was a brief pause. Then Claudine asked, "What brings you here?"

"You! I want to...to be like you. To try to be...."

The irony was not lost on Claudine. For Emilie to arrive from one side of the bridge with all those memories and connections, to ask her help to thrive at the opposite side, and just when Claudine was hoping for something to tip the balance. Was a slightly lopsided Emilie, a less-than-perfect Emilie a sign?

Claudine took a deep breath anticipating all the things she wanted to say, when Emilie made a request that resounded in Claudine's already-cluttered mind: "Show me Claudine the..."

"You mean...."

"The human!"

Claudine hesitated. Did not Emilie realize that she, Claudine, was about to star in a motion picture as her ladybug self? Surely that self was a wondrous thing? She struggled, then acceded. These days it took only the merest nod from Pierre, and Claudine was on her own, able to change at will. It seemed that, with the transformation came the klieg lights. Was it the sun? The reflection of light from the river, below? The glow of Claudine, self-generated? Wherever it came from, it was undeniable.

For suddenly a beautiful young lady of the biped variety was standing on the bridge, Emilie on one hand, Pierre holding the other. If he didn't love her, he would describe her as quite the

Chapter III

catch.

Emilie was electrified: "Oh, my! Yes! You are like that garden at the Palais de la Reine. Remember? We all vowed to look, but never intrude. Remember? That's you!"

"But Emilie, you are...attractive, too! Perhaps some two-tone sneakers would help you...?" Pierre looked at her in astonishment. Claudine would never be caught in such footwear. She continued, "We don't have to change like....like this to be successful. I just look different. Pretty comes in many ways. Like you said, the flowers."

A perhaps too tainted admonition, so, to no avail. Emilie spoke to Pierre. Pleaded, really. "Can you make me like Claudine is now? Can you? I know you know the way! I..."

Pierre cut her off: "Yes, you need this! Change is my business. But once the change has been made, the rest is up to you. Closing time is closing time." He turned to Claudine: "It's time to go."

Claudine, still in her human form, unhappily agreed. She watched them leave.

Four
THE SOLDIER

A handsome soldier appeared on the bridge. Back from the front lines and a brief stay in a field hospital, he needed a cane to keep himself upright and steady. Leaning on the sculpted railing of the bridge that crossed the Seine, he watched the waters that luckily had no similarity to those of the ocean he had just crossed.

"I...." he began. Claudine's human loveliness obviated language. "You...." she said, and glanced at his uniform, and his cane.

He looked down at the water, at the stones that made-up the bridge, at her.. "This is like a dream. After what I saw...After what I lived....How can so much beauty exist in the same world? Or was I in a different world?"

Claudine looked at the soldier's uncertain reflection. He seemed lost, though how he was lost, she could not determine.

Chapter IV

He said, "'Like a Poet hidden in the light of thought.' From a poem by Shelley. I don't know why, but when I look at you, I think, I wonder…." He wandered a bit internally, having lost his footing, then said, "In your eyes, I think you know what it means to be hidden in light…"

Claudine thought of sunlight on flower petals and spotlights on runways and feeling that she truly was hidden. She had felt lonely. Adulation was not seeing, And it did not relieve loneliness. Standing next to this fellow was no coincidence; it was Fate, as any creature of Nature would know.

Time seemed to slow down. Even the water around the bridge only suggested motion out of obligation, though the waters, too, seemed caught in this Time-dilation. The soldier saw the reminder of clouds in their surface, which caused him to ask Claudine:

"Have you ever flown?"

"I…I can only imagine."

"I have. I can," he said.

"Don't you need wings?"

The soldier pointed to his chest. "I have them." There were the wings of the Airmen among his various ribbons. "I earned them. Reconnaissance. Even with four engines, you can sense the quiet – see the quiet – around you. The freedom. Imagine! Being lost in a cloud, being above it. No limits up or down!"

Claudine knew this feeling well.

The soldier looked at her beside him, and knew she was both inches and miles away.

Looking into the waters below, Claudine watched the

motions and wondered if there were patterns, meanings to them, or if they had a shared goal in mind as they interacted, or at least bumped into each other.

She recalled a time when she and her friends, Hannah, Belle and Tony the Cricket were relaxing under the cool sun, the snow around them shrinking away, when Spring arrived quite unexpectedly. They were happy to see her.

She smiled and said, "It's almost time."

Every animal, every tree, and every blade of grass heard her and pulsated with anticipation.

Tony said, "Spring!" His legs almost sprung as he said the word.

But Hannah and Belle felt otherwise. "Ugh. Spring. Nothing personal, Spring, but you know what that means: Humans! Running all over the place. Stepping on us, smashing us, cutting and clipping, driving us out so they can spread themselves all over! Give me Winter! Quiet. Privacy. Distance!" The others nodded, except for Tony, who was smart enough to remain silent.

Claudine pondered prophetically, "I wonder what those human creatures think of us. Dropping into their tea. Getting caught in their clothes...."

She shivered when she remembered those words: "Getting caught in their clothes." She thought, "That's the story of my life!" and laughed.

The soldier smiled at the magic of that sound, her laughter. Claudine saw him smiling, and said – cryptically to him – "And here I am, caught again."

Chapter IV

That was the narrative in her mind. Looking into his eyes, at his leg, his cane, another story, a new story was forming, one not of nets and knits, but of someone else's release and winged freedom.

Five
CLAUDINE GOES AWAY

Claudine went to Pierre's apartment.

"I have to leave for a while," she said.

"The soldier. I see."

"No," she said truthfully.

"You will return soon, all the same? The film opening..."

"I don't know," said Claudine.

"Promise me that you will remain human in your travels. To be safer, yes? Well."

She would not remind him that she had made it all the way to Paris alone, as her ladybug self, traveling by train, by foot, until she had found his shop of shoes and transformation.

"I will remain human," she acquiesced, "for as long as I can."

As she left the apartment, a feather fell from the sky and landed at her feet. Was it pointing in a specific, deliberate direction? A bit of detritus from a molting friend, or a gloriously ambiguous divine symbol?

Six
THE TREE AND THE OTTER

Claudine, the lady, walked the streets of Paris, not knowing where she was headed. She had almost passed that famous bookstore on the left bank, when she noticed in the window a poster declaiming the words, *"Who is Claudine?"* It was advertising for a mystery book by R.M. Hamilton, set in the Australian highlands. "Surely another book about me," thought Claudine, and she turned to enter the store when the heel of her shoe caught on a cobblestone and she fell forward, thinking "Perhaps I should write a book," and then all went dark. When she awoke, she was in a forest.

It was not a place that existed in Paris. She heard a sound like a sigh, turned again, and was face to face with Glyndynshout, the Otter.

"I'm glad you're here," he said. He took her hand and hurried her to a tree, whence that sigh had come.

Dee Prinkles The Oak was one-hundred and sixty-three years old. She relished life. So, what was her concern? Why were her branches hanging just a bit lower, this year? Why did her leaves, still lush, show the slightest curl at their edges? And her bark – that tells-all and hides-nothing persona - why the weariness in its role as its tree's armor?

Dee spoke to them as if lost in thought, perhaps reminiscing: "I am here by happenstance." Glyndynshout wanted to ask her to define "here," but he held himself. She went on: "I was a seed once, long ago...Not so long ago if you ask the moon, or that mountain behind me. A seed caught briefly by a paw, then stuck to a talon, then packed into a boot, and finally brought to this very place by a puff of wind caused by the swing of a leopard's tail. Here, where years don't matter. Where years don't exist unless you want them to. But something has brushed against my being...."

Glyndynshout looked at Claudine: He whispered to her, "What to do? What to say? Is this a real ailment?" Dee heard and said, "Real! A bit of wind from a leopard's tail. Think about it: isn't that precisely how we all ended up here?"

Claudine said, "No... I was walking the streets of Paris and saw a book about me and then I fell..."

'How do we question how," interrupted the tree, "when here we are?" Dee knew she had to pause to allow them to consider the million million variables that led to this precise place... as if this place were precise! The audacity of such a thought!

"And I thought I was lost!" cried the otter.

Dee said, "You had to be lost in order to be found. Claudine's presence on that bridge... Oh, yes, I know the story..."

Chapter VI

Glyndynshout dared to say, "We have the same story, it seems."

Dee said, "I could have ended up anywhere."

"Not according to your story. Considering all those things that determined your direction, you could have landed nowhere else," said the otter. "Now that I think of it, the same with me. Maybe with all of us."

"What if I had ended up somewhere else? asked Dee. "What if I ended up being a picnic table?"

"Then we'd be talking to a picnic table."

Dee glowed.

Claudine was bewildered by this exchange. What did it mean? What did it have to do with her? It occurred to Claudine that she could do worse than stay there and try to understand this exchange; but in the next moment she found herself thanking the tree and announcing her intention to take a walk. She set off, with Glyndynshout pattering alongside her.

The lady and the otter came to one of the myriad crossroads in the Forest. Said Glyndynshout, "I think I know who can help you with... something. Something that might come up." He pointed. "You see this path? Only so far. Then the path disappears, Maybe it's a rule: you're only allowed to see so far."

If Claudine were in her other form, she would have taken wing, not to fly away, but to try to see farther down the path. There's a price to pay for the human form: you have to trade in your wings for two legs that often did not lead *anywhere*.

Seven
PIERRE

Pierre raised his eyes from *Descarte's Le Géométrie*. The window did not show the rain, but the sound of it on the roof and on the leaves made him think of angles and randomness and intentionality. To believe that every drop had been predetermined, perhaps eons ago, wishing the world were compatible with the symphony of symbols, wishing he knew the intentions of the image seemingly wavering before him. Where had she gone? The world he had prepared her for, the world that she wanted, did not presently hold her. Claudine, he knew, was not one for whimsy; perhaps, then, he could generate some rational formula that would lead him to her. As familiar as Pierre was with instincts and impulses, he often felt that resorting to reason and logic could yield the desired solution.

Pierre had wrestled with her absence for - how long? Was

Chapter VII

it only two weeks? Needing relief, he had turned to math: the secret language that, once comprehended, showed you, not a new world, but the same world through the lens of a lens of a lens.

He laughed. Perhaps it was the sough of the wind or drops of rain knocking at the glass for attention, but he thought of the wonderland of this world of numbers. He thought of zero. Is zero real or imaginary? Rational or irrational? He laughed when he would say to himself, "Simply replace the word 'zero' with the word 'Claudine'" – for the world and Claudine were now synonymous to him – and see the answers.

Pierre took a sip of wine and rose to look through the window. Not so far away, the stone urn that she used to fill with flowers stood on the balcony, darkened by the rain, and empty.

Eight
MARRAKESH, MOROCCO, MAGICAL FOREST

Claudine sat in a lounge chair by a pool in the Hotel Dulcet and pondered her two legs, two feet and pedicured toes. Below the chair rested her sandals. She thought about how much of a human's body was devoted to legs. By her guess, half. Certainly not the same ratio when considering her former ladybug figure.

Perhaps it was the scent of flowers or the gentle movements of the air which her original self could not only discern, but could differentiate and parse: To read the breeze like a song, note for note; to be able to disassemble and reassemble those gentle motions. She couldn't wait any longer. Claudine would allow Nature's songs to support and carry her, to move her by wing or by foot, to disembark whenever she chose.

The other hotel guests reclining on chairs or floating in the

Chapter VIII

enormous pool noticed that where this strikingly lovely woman had been sitting there now sat a pair of sunglasses and a beach towel.

Claudine was in her glory; so happy, she was crying, and so sad, she had to laugh. Claudine The Ladybug was being carried by the wind, her wings open, the world gliding beneath her. She spotted a garden of flowers and asserted her wings to bring her there, and once there, she found a beautiful lush green leaf on which to land. She almost sank into its cushiony surface. Her legs secured her and she fell asleep, the gentle wind humming a lullaby to assure her rest.

"*Bonjour, ma chère petite coccinelle.* Thank you for visiting my garden."

Claudine opened her eyes. "You," she began.. "You are here!"

"I am," said Yves. "I live here."

She looked around. A wall of impossible blue, marble pools, bougainvilleas, the scent of jasmine... and deep shade, cool and luxuriant within the heat of Morocco. It was the *Jardin Majorelle.*

"I needed to run away," said the patron saint of Parisian fashion. "To be a kid again. Will you play with me?"

Claudine looked at his lean, sad face, the famous dark-rimmed glasses.

He went on, "I will never forget the Paris years.... To begin again, to begin - that is the point, isn't it? Never mind where in the order of things. Will you play, Mademoiselle Ladybug?"

'I am Claudine," she said. "Of course I will!"

Yves smiled. "I went outside today, and despite the heat, I smelled spring, So of course you are here!"

For the next few hours, they sketched, and sewed, and sipped tea, and talked.

"I have a Pierre, too," he told her. "He's been with me through my many discoveries, my illness...he was always present...For me, *ma chère*, the real magic was the first magic."

At last Claudine was in a fetching new dress - "Perfect for your charming figure" - an A-line creation, with a round, flat collar, and long tied bow. She wore heels (*bien sûr!*) and a small, round-brimmed hat. Yves applauded. "You are perfect, my darling friend."

Claudine loved her new look, then stopped herself and said, "Ah, I love this too much."

"No!" cried Yves. "The way you dress, the way you make yourself even more beautiful is not vanity, it is your gift to us - to me - you let me play! Who would begrudge the bestower of such gifts?" Yves spread his arms to encompass the world as he wanted it to be. "Anyone else doesn't count!"

Claudine laughed, and agreed, and looked around at Yves' garden. "Who designed all this? It belongs, don't you see? There is no chaos here. It all fits, can you see?"

Now Yves laughed. "*Ma belle*, now you are talking about yourself!"

Nine

Pierre in the Forest

Pierre was a man of great patience, and a rooster of even greater forbearance. As most creatures know, roosters are not known for their laid-back, low-key characters. Yet, though it hadn't been long at all, an urgency settled on his missing Claudine. He realized, in her absence, that he was indeed ready to put all his eggs in one basket. And there is no excuse for that sentence.

He grabbed his hat from the rack at the store's entrance, and headed to the only place that could be his sanctuary, his haven in all of his transfigurations: the Magical Forest. He knew the path with his eyes closed, and so, with his hat pulled so low it did cover his eyes, he took those steps to get him to that breezy, shaded place where Elephant and Rabbit were known to lounge and discourse. And, lo!

Rabbit was happy to see him, a fellow thinker and knower, two very different things, almost opposite things, as thinkers come to know. "*Pierre! Mon ami! Comment ça va?*"

"Rabbit, my friend. And dear Elephant! How are you?"

"We're pretty good," said Rabbit. "But you, sir, are here for a reason."

Pierre presented the situation: "You have known me in many forms. I have sought the one that fits me best and I believe I have found it. Living in Paris serves me well and certainly helped me make up my mind. I met there a splendid....no, perfect...my heart! Goodness, my heart!"

"Congratulations! So what's the catch?"

"Her name is Claudine. She, too, sought another life, and she, too, transformed herself – abetted by your humble weaver – but I believe she is less decided about her choice than I was. She left Paris... I asked her to remain human. I am being selfish; I do not wish to lose her. She is by nature, a ladybug - the sweetest, most delightful..."

Rabbit smiled. "Let me ask you a question: Is there any pairing less conceivable or more ridiculous than a friendship between a Rabbit and an Elephant?"

Pierre said: "Friends, yes. And I could be her friend. But I wish so much more for us. Romance, I believe, is the right context."

"That's funny," said Rabbit, smiling broadly.

Pierre took exception and asked, "Why 'funny'?"

Rabbit pointed with his left ear. Coming down the path was Claudine the Ladybug. Rabbit was a bigger believer in Paths

Chapter IX

than others in the Forest. As far as Rabbit was concerned, Paths know what they're doing. At least, in the Magical Forest. In other locales, one should be more circumspect.

She was beautiful in her new ensemble and ladybug colors.

Pierre, entirely out of character, ran toward her and would have picked her up and kissed her, had not Glyndnshout appeared and held up a warning paw. "*Non, monsieur,*" he said. "Not yet." Pierre saw the look in his eyes, urgent and knowing, and hung back.

Ten
CLAUDINE AND THE FOREST

Evening was coming; the posture of the sun and its insistence on attention were waning as it allowed itself to be an orange disk in a blue sky surmounting the treetops, making room for his sister, the Moon. Claudine saw the sun as a spotlight, a limelight. She felt so stunning in her new outfit, she imagined that the Forest gave her a standing ovation; every creature, every leaf, stood in silence to show their admiration, even adoration of her spectacular beauty. There was no jealousy on their part, she thought; no envy, none of that green-eyed-monster nonsense; just the acknowledgment of her magical presence. Her clothes enhanced her loveliness, exactly as the sky enhanced the hills; the lakes enhanced the trees; the trees enhanced the variegated and variously-textured land; the shadows enhanced the influence of the breeze. Call it the

Chapter X

choreography of Nature.

"It is a dance, a dance! I am your prima ballerina," -she laughed and twirled - "and all of the Forest is my *corps de ballet!*" After that statement, there was an intensity of rustling which Claudine took as applause; but Glyndynshout, wishing to prevent a storm, hurriedly took her hands and whispered, "Trees are touchy! Remember Dee?" He pulled her into a kind of *pas de deux* which took them on through the Forest. A path divided itself into two directions, and one of them – at least – was carpeted in red.

Claudine paused. A long one.

Eleven
The Test

There was a pond, which was hardly unusual in this place. The water was so still, so serene, it was almost begging to be disturbed by the images of troubled creatures seeking solace. Not to disappoint, the ladybug and the otter looked into -or onto – the mirror of water. Silently, they gazed.

Quiet like that is destined to be interrupted. From directly behind them, they heard a man say, "Stunning!" And stunned they were; the two turned to see another couple examining them imperiously. Pierre, hidden from view, knew them immediately; they were the king and queen of the Fashion World, Adam Endive and Eveline Sans Coeur, dressed as if about to attend a royal gala. They were the paragons of supernal style.

"My dear, my dear, " said Eveline, "you are the work of a genius! So close to perfection, I almost deigned to shed a tear for

Chapter XI

the stopping at one half-step too soon."

Adam spoke, "But, my dear, you are in luck! For you have found your Pygmalion. We shall make you perfect! We shall make you immortal for your loveliness to be venerated for eternity by all those who wish to see something so rare: perfection made manifest!"

Glynynshout dared to speak. "Madam..."

Eveline cut him off. "Otter! Your reputation precedes you! Truly, to the very word, *friend*." Then her tone changed from complimentary to admonitory: "But make no mistake: we shall take this magnificent ladybug and sculpt her to perfection and she shall take up residence in our garden. A centerpiece among our other masterpieces. But there she shall remain: Perfect, but not yours."

Turning to Claudine, she asked, "What say you, young Claudine? You shall be the envy of every eye; you shall be in perpetual pose, created solely to be admired. Never to be touched! For no one shall be worthy to even brush a finger on your silk gown. Even the wind will be too shy to risk an inadvertent contouring of your garb. We say again: mere mention of your name shall render red carpets sere. Brown, threadbare, like stubble on the chin of an aged sailor."

Perfect and perpetual. A work of art utterly without the soul that held her heart. Even, perhaps, without a soul at all. A lovely, lonely sculpture. Claudine clung to Glyndynshout's arm with both hands.

Twelve
SELINE

The moon rose prematurely, giving the sun, just getting ready to clock-out anyway, a little nudge. (The Night Manager was flexible about stuff like this; she knew things would not spiral out of control; the sun and the moon were very reasonable characters; meteors and comets, on the other hand...) The moon was waxing toward fullness. (Aren't we all?) But she wanted to put in her two cents' worth. She (we'll call her Selene) had been in Claudine's shoes. Zeus lusted after her, Pan flat-out loved her, and if you wanted to see a woman display her robes and dazzle the universe, she was your model. Pan was able to convince – charm, captivate - her to take up residence in the woods of Arcadia. Eventually, she came to her senses, shrugged her shoulders, and conceded to herself that she was not meant to bide her time in the lustrous groves and copses in the

Chapter XII

restful shade of the forest, but to adjust the light of the night sky as was her fashion and charge. Yes, even the gods have responsibilities that they must adhere to, or at least should adhere to, allowing an occasional lapse. And, boy, do we humans adore those rare exceptions; we practically worship them.

Selene spoke to Claudine in her ear. As Claudine stood perfectly still, Glyndynshout sensed something of enormous significance and took a step back, instinctively knowing not to interfere.

The moon whispered in a way that made the words seem to be formed from breezes. "Ah, Claudine. You have been given some wonderful gifts: you have been given yourself and your talents – blessings; you have been given the love of Pierre, and that of a new friend, the otter; and the incomparable gift of seeing and hearing and knowing this strange, unpredictable planet that for secret reasons makes you search for its magic, whether in rocks, or seas, or birds or humans. Oh, savor these morsels of priceless nourishment. Forfeit none of these for that which is the curse attendant to vanity: an existence of lifeless perfection."

Claudine could hear the moon's smile in her voice when she said, "Trust me, you have been allotted enough time." (Ah, if one could imagine the moon rolling her eyes to accompany these words.) She added, "And, *ma chère*, you will always be Claudine."

Maman? thought Claudine. *You are here? Oh, Maman...*

No...surely it was the moon...

She looked up at Selene, her glowing light, and she

compared that to the footlights and klieg lights and flashbulbs that blinded one foolish enough to look directly at them. How light could be so different! Lights that beckon and embrace; lights that trespass and expose and unnerve. Claudine, lucky creature, saw the value of both - wisely parsed. And there, a never to be extinguished truth.

Glyndynshout sat with her until she slept. When she awoke, he pointed to a path.

"Thank you," said Claudine. "I think I know the way." He followed her nonetheless. A flower at his feet looked up at him in annoyance. "It wasn't supposed to *rain* tonight," she said. "You're mussing my petals."

"Flowers are worse than trees," he said, wiping his eyes. Claudine laughed gently, and held his paw; then she turned; then another turn...and she was in Paris. It was still daylight there.

Thirteen
Claudine Returns

Walking down the quiet, familiar street, Claudine found the establishment of the Tailor of Transformation, and walked in. The tiny bell tingled, but Pierre did not have to look up from his work to know who had entered. And one did not have to see his face to know the glorious smile that appeared or feel the contentment that filled all his iterations simultaneously, when he knew she was home.

As they sauntered along the path to the bridge, a bird landed in front of them. A handsome bluebird with unusually bright plumage, he moved towards them. Claudine noticed that this marvelous avian favored one leg, as if with a limp. The bird stopped, smiled and spoke. "Thank you," is all he said before he took wing and disappeared over the treetops.

"Pierre!"

"You wanted me to help him, yes? You are pleased?" asked Pierre. "I just want to make creatures happy. To help them.".

"I am pleased," said Claudine, examining her heart. The airman looked happy: he could fly again. She had helped someone. She hadn't fallen in love with him, and counted herself lucky. It could have been so much worse. "He loved me when I was human," she thought. "He might not have even seen me as a ladybug. Some creatures are like that, it seems."

She looked at Pierre, who knew her in all her forms, who had watched but never interfered with her growth through her many discoveries, yet was always present.

The first magic was the real magic.

Fourteen
The Premiere

One week later. It was the opening night of Claudine's movie, *Brief Candle*, and the theater was glowing from the marquee and the lights radiating from photographers and the luminous celebrities and dignitaries from all walks of life strutting their radiant way into the playhouse. The parade was nothing less than VIPyrotechnics.

Yet, when Claudine emerged onto the red carpet with Pierre on her arm, it seemed as if Time had stopped. Even the veterans of such events were frozen in their tracks when they saw the unapproachable, incomparable, almost supernatural presence of this ladybug, whose beauty and talent were deemed worthy of the likes of Garbo, Deneuve, and Marion Cotillard. Her name echoed in the voices of fans and photographers.

She began to laugh and Pierre knew why. She said, "I feel

like showing my wings!"

Pierre laughed, too. "Polka dots and wings! I'm not sure the world is ready for such a statement!" He half-consciously tucked a bit of feather back into his perfectly-measured and meticulously-pressed sleeve. (Nature can really get under your skin.)

With a big smile much appreciated by the paparazzi, Claudine said to her love, "This," and she made a dramatic wave with her gloved hand, "is a very nice place to visit...."

There was no need for Pierre to finish her sentence. He just waved to the crowd. It was that pose, that smiling, happy gesture that made it to the front page the next day.

Fifteen
Another Week Later...

Claudine, ladybug forevermore, left her apartment in the sixth arrondissement and headed straight for the first. She was wearing a trench coat and dark glasses, and carried a tote containing a parcel wrapped in brown paper. Walking along the rue de Rivoli, passing the cafes and *boulangeries*, she would not stop for *croissants* or the morning baguette, or even for her favorite *pain au chocolat. Non.* Not today. She did not pause until she saw the exterior of the Louvre. Finding the correct entrance, she walked through the grand gallery, where Napoleon III and Marie Louise led a procession on the occasion of their wedding. It was in the Salon Carré that Claudine stopped.

She opened her tote and unwrapped the parcel, taking out also a hammer and a nail...

It was quiet that morning in the Louvre, and a guard heard the tiny tapping. He turned and saw a ladybug - a ravishing one, he might add - hanging a portrait of herself on the museum wall. All his life he would remember that moment, when something like champagne bubbled up within him and overflowed into a delight he would never feel again. Claudine finished her task. The guard caught her eye, smiled, tipped his hat, and bowed. He had seen her movie, and approved. Claudine smiled back and waved, as if she were on the red carpet, and he, an adoring fan - which he was, oh, my dears, he was!

The End

Acknowledgements

Ruth Marie Hamilton, for writing "The Clockwork Giant", a mystery story set in the Australian Highlands. It features our first Claudine book and includes the chapter, "Who is Claudine?" You can find Ruth's story on her blog, meandthebfg.com by clicking on the tab "Kid's Stories". She illustrates her own children's books, which are sweet, funny, and slightly edgy: in other words, irresistible. Ruth can be found on Facebook and Instagram, and all of her books are available through Amazon or at ZealAus Publishing.

Stacie Flint, for painting "The Beauty Slave's Quest for Serenity" - the portrait of a distraught woman that inspired one of the themes of our book. Her surprising use of color first drew me to her paintings, and I stayed for their depth of soul. You can find Stacie on Facebook and Instagram, and at her website www.stacieflint.com.

Fabienne Ruiz, for her charming quote about ladybugs. Fabienne is a watercolor artist and an illustrator of children's books. She is on Facebook and Instagram and her adorable work can be found at www.verteplumeeditions.com

Fabienne Ruiz, pour sa charmante citation à propos des coccinelles. Fabienne est aquarelliste et illustratrice des livres d'enfant. Elle est sur Facebook et Instagram, et on peut trouver ses adorables créations à Verte Plume Éditions.

Special thanks to **Andria Budd**, for her loving support, her willingness to listen, and her unfailing good taste.

      - Marian Grudko

Thanks to **Andrew Marvell**, **Ecclesiastes**, **Ferlinghetti**, **Beckett**, and **Arthur Rimbaud**, who got the drift. **And to the rest of the gang:** I am grateful.

      -T.A. Young

Also by the authors

Marian Grudko

Claudine: A Fairy Tale for Exceptional Grownups

Lucinda Snowdrop

T.A. Young

Claudine: A Fairy Tale for Exceptional Grownups

Elephant and Rabbit As Told By Skib Bricluster

Elephant and Rabbit and Skib

The Fairy Tale Book of Bifford C. Wellington

Praise for Claudine: A Fairy Tale for Exceptional Grownups

...deep and fun, with hilarious remarks on the Paris world, cafes, Fashion Week...lots of plays on words and fun interjections... The book seems at first glance to be for children, but as the title highlights, this is actually a fairy tale for grownups - who may need a few life lessons...

- Emma Cazabonne, wordsandpeace.com

Printed in the USA
CPSIA information can be obtained
at www.ICGtesting.com
LVHW071902091124
795957LV00004BA/101